epic! originals

DIARY OF A 5TH GRADE
OUTLAW
THE FRIEND THIEF

GINA LOVELESS

ILLUSTRATIONS BY
ANDREA BELL

Andrews McMeel
PUBLISHING®

DIARY OF A 5TH GRADE OUTLAW:
THE FRIEND THIEF

Andrews McMeel Publishing
a division of Andrews McMeel Universal
1130 Walnut Street, Kansas City, Missouri 64106

www.andrewsmcmeel.com

Epic! Creations, Inc.
702 Marshall Street, Suite 280, Redwood City, California 94063

www.getepic.com

20 21 22 23 24 SDB 10 9 8 7 6 5 4 3 2 1

ISBN: 978-1-5248-5574-1

Library of Congress Control Number: 2019951259

Design by Dan Nordskog

Made by:
King Yip (Dongguan) Printing & Packaging Factory Ltd.
Address and location of manufacturer:
Daning Administrative District, Humen Town
Dongguan Guangdong, China 523930
1st Printing—1/20/20

ATTENTION: SCHOOLS AND BUSINESSES
Andrews McMeel books are available at quantity discounts with
bulk purchase for educational, business, or sales promotional
use. For information, please e-mail the Andrews McMeel
Publishing Special Sales Department:
specialsales@amuniversal.com.

SATURDAY, OCTOBER 5

So, something kinda . . . off happened today. Like when you brush your teeth before eating breakfast and then you take a big swig of orange juice, and you're like, "Aww, man, why do I keep doing this to myself?"

At first, I was with a whole bunch of my friends and we were all playing basketball. Unless someone handed me five meatball subs and said, "Here, these are free, and they're for you and your friends," I couldn't imagine a better day.

It was nice to just play ball and be drama-free after last week. So much crazy stuff had happened!

1. I thought I'd lost my best friend, Mary Ann, forever.
2. I made friends with a girl named LJ.

3. LJ and I stood up to Nadia, the school bully.

4. I got to know Sammy, Allana, and Dale.

5. The whole school got into a huge mud fight. Partly because of me.

LJ must have felt the same way, because she invited me, Sammy, Allana, and Dale to hang out at her house today. For the first few hours it rained, so we watched this movie called *The Goonies*. It's about a bunch of kids who follow this pirate map and go on some crazy adventures. LJ's mom even got us a bunch of Baby Ruth chocolate bars to snack on because that's the candy bar they eat in the movie! (I love any movie that has a sweet treat in it!)

Then it got all bright and shiny out, and LJ and I looked at each other and said, "basketball?" at the same time. LJ asked her mom if we could go to the park near her house, and she said it was okay, but she made LJ's big brother, Darien, come with us.

LJ and I love to compete with each other at basketball because we're the two best players at our school. Allana and Dale haven't played much b-ball, so LJ and

Allana were one team and Dale and I were the other. Sammy thinks basketball is boring, but he knows a lot about it because his older sister plays it, so he volunteered to be the referee. Darien thinks basketball is even more boring than Sammy does, so he just sat on a swing, playing on his phone.

Even though we were on the court and LJ was on the foul line, getting ready to shoot her free throw, I kept thinking about *The Goonies*. I felt like my group of friends was just like those kids.

Before LJ could shoot, I said,
"I think we should come up with
a name for our group. Everyone
knows I'm The Outlaw—"

"Do they?" Sammy asked.

"Yeah, I'm pretty sure everyone
calls you Robin Hood now," LJ said.

"It's like, 50 percent The Outlaw, 50 percent Robin Hood," I said.

"More like 99 percent Robin Hood," Allana said.

"And 1 percent Robin Loxley," Dale said.

They all laughed, and I had to laugh with them.

You see, our school has a reward system called Bonus Bucks where you can earn bucks toward cool privileges. But this girl Nadia had set up a tax and charged bucks to do anything on the playground, which was super unfair. So last week, LJ and I had rescued every Bonus Buck from Nadia's desk.

We had returned the bucks to all the kids in school, along with a note from The 5th Grade Outlaw.

I thought the name Outlaw would stick, but during a big showdown where I played one-on-one basketball against this meanie Ty Lisborn, kids started cheering for Robin Hood. I guess they called me that because I'm always wearing a hoodie.

Now everyone calls me that. I tried saying, "Hey, what about Basketball Goddess?" but, yeah— they didn't go for that, either.

"Anyway," I said while laughing, "I just think it would be cool to have a name for our group. That's all."

"It would be cool if I could make this shot," LJ said with a big grin.

I laughed a little harder. "I'm sorry, I'm sorry. Go ahead. We can talk about it later."

LJ flicked her wrist, the ball arced through the air, and then *SWISH*—it went right through the hoop.

"Good shot!" a bright voice said.

I turned around and saw Mary Ann walking toward us. I ran right off the court and over to her.

"Ready?" I asked.

"Ready!" she said.

That's when Mary Ann and

I did our awesome handshake,
which looks a little like this:

There were still three more moves before the handshake was completely finished.

By then, nobody was on the basketball court. They had gathered around Mary Ann and me.

"What are you doing?" LJ asked.

"Our super special handshake," Mary Ann said. "We used to do it every morning before class."

"But now that we don't have class together, we do it whenever we see each other outside of school," I said.

"That's so cool!" Allana said.

"Can you teach it to us?" Dale asked.

"Sure," I said.

For the next few minutes, Mary Ann and I did our handshake over and over while Allana and Dale copied it and then tried out their own moves.

At one point, I looked over at LJ. She was looking at her watch and then back over at the basketball court.

That's when I remembered that we'd totally been in the middle of a game!

"Oh jeez!" I said. "Hey, guys, we should get back on the court!"

LJ smiled and nodded. "Let's finish the game," she said and

ran over to get the ball.

"Can I play?" Mary Ann asked.

"Sure," I said. "We were playing two on two, but you can totally join. You can be on my team, and Sammy can be on their team."

"No," Sammy said. "No way. Not interested."

"Come on, Sammy, please?" LJ asked. "Otherwise, we can't play."

Sammy's cheeks turned pink. "Oh, all right."

At first, the game was going good. I forgot that Mary Ann doesn't really play basketball, so LJ stole the ball away from her really easily. But Mary Ann totally ran back after it. LJ's just so fast, Mary Ann couldn't catch up. LJ passed the ball to Allana, who was by the right side of the backboard.

Allana took her shot, but she missed, and it bounced off the backboard.

LJ leapt and caught the ball just as Mary Ann reached her. As LJ went for the rebound, Mary Ann jumped up. Her hands collided with LJ's arms and the ball fell to the ground.

That's when everything started feeling off.

"That's a foul," Sammy said.

"You're not the ref anymore," I said. "And she didn't know."

"He's right," LJ said. "That's still a foul. We get a free throw."

I don't know why, but what they said bugged me. It felt like they were picking on Mary Ann. "Just let it go," I said. "She didn't know. And now that she does, she won't do it again."

LJ threw her hands up high. Mary Ann picked up the ball and passed it to Sammy.

"It's okay, Robin. I don't mind," Mary Ann said.

Sammy passed the ball to LJ, who dribbled it over to the foul line.

Allana and Sammy cheered her on. Even Dale was saying, "You can do it!"

But I knew LJ would make the shot, so I looked across the court at Mary Ann and made a silly face at her. I pretended I was eating a chicken leg and it was too hot.

Mary Ann giggled. She pretended to cut up food on a plate and eat it.

I burst out laughing.

I guess my timing wasn't too good, because the laugh spilled out of me and surprised LJ just as she took her shot. That meant that instead of it going in, the ball hit the backboard and bounced off.

I probably should have apologized to LJ for messing up her free throw. But instead, I just kept laughing and miming silly things with Mary Ann.

Which meant I also didn't go after the ball once it bounced off the backboard.

I guess Dale did, because he threw the ball at me. But I wasn't paying attention, and it flew right past.

Or at least I *think* it did, because Dale yelled, "Robin!" and then LJ ran by me, got the ball, dribbled it a little farther back, and shot it.

SWISH!

That's when Mary Ann said, "All this fake eating is making me hungry!"

I walked over and put my arm around Mary Ann's shoulder. "I'm usually the one who's always hungry!"

Mary Ann looked over toward the parking lot. Her mom was inside her car, checking her watch. She motioned for Mary Ann that it was time to go.

"Hey," Mary Ann whispered. "Do you want to come to my house for dinner?"

My smile grew to the size of a birthday cake. Mary Ann hadn't invited me over to her house since we'd become friends again.

That was only about a week ago, but still.

I looked back at the group. They were all standing in a circle on the court.

I felt a little bad leaving, but I had spent *all day* with them. I was pretty sure they wouldn't mind if I went to Mary Ann's.

I called my mom to make sure it was okay. When I nodded to Mary Ann, her smile got as big as a watermelon.

Then Mary Ann ran over to her mom.

I decided to tell my friends I was leaving. I told them as fast as I could. Like, so fast that all of the words were actually parts of one big word.

"Hey-guys-Mary-Ann-invited-me-to-dinner-and-I-said-yes-so-I'm-going-to-go-this-was-fun-I'll-see-you-guys-at-school-on-Monday."

At first, they all blinked and stared at me like my face was covered in pink frosting and they weren't sure if it was strawberry or bubblegum flavored.

But then Sammy, Allana, and Dale all came over and high-fived me.

And then the weird thing I mentioned at the beginning of this diary entry...well, that's when it happened. I stood there, waiting to hear LJ say, "See ya later," but she didn't say goodbye to me. She didn't even look at me. Instead, she knelt down and tried to get something off the bottom of her shoe.

I didn't know what to do, so I waved to everybody else, ran over to the car, and got in the back seat next to Mary Ann.

"Mom, would you mind if we didn't have pizza?" Mary Ann asked. "I know we usually have pizza on Saturdays, but Robin doesn't really like pizza. Could we have something else, like spaghetti and meatballs, or maybe tuna casserole, or ..."

But I don't really know what else Mary Ann said, because I was looking out the window, back at my other friends. They were all headed back to the court, except for LJ. She was looking back at me like she still couldn't tell what flavor that frosting was on my face.

As Mary Ann's mom drove away, my stomach sank into my feet. I put my hood up. What was going on with LJ?

CHAPTER 2

MONDAY, OCTOBER 7

During the whole drive over to Mary Ann's, I tried to get the look LJ gave me out of my head.

I couldn't shake it in the car, but it was pretty easy once we landed at Mary Ann's house. Especially when dinner turned into a sleepover. And a pretty epic one at that:

My mom picked me up on Sunday, and all day long I was grinning about what a great time I'd had at Mary Ann's.

In fact, when I showed up to school this morning, I was still thinking about it. Then I walked into Ms. Gaffey's classroom and saw LJ sitting at her desk. Everything that happened on the court on Saturday flashed back into my head.

I put my hood up and went over to my desk. I took my books out of my backpack and looked back at LJ really quick.

She smiled at me, and I breathed a huge sigh of relief. Maybe nothing had been wrong with LJ after all. Maybe Saturday had just been a big mix-up in my head, like when I watch a show with my parents and they laugh at a joke, but I don't get it. (That happens *all* the time. I do *not* get Mom and Dad's sense of humor!)

Anyway, I put my hood back down.

"Are you going to the school fair on Wednesday?" LJ asked.

"You know it!" I said.

"I'm in, too!" Sammy shouted from a few desks over.

Allana and Dale looked at each other and nodded their heads. This meant they were about to do one of their signature raps. Dale started, and Allana went next.

The school fair
> *Is coming to town*
It'll turn the school
> *Upside down*
There's basketball
> *And Whac-A-Mole*
And a dunk tank
> *With the principal!*
There's ring toss
> *Where you win a fish*
And plate break
> *Where you crack a dish*
But the reason we

Go to the fair
Is to stuff our stomachs
Like we just don't care!
We'll eat caramel corn
And hot dogs
Until we're croaking
Like two bullfrogs!

Everybody clapped at the end of their rhyme. It was one of their best ones yet.

Even Nadia clapped because honestly, who doesn't love the fair?

I clapped, too. Then I clapped my hand to my stomach. All that talk of hot dogs and caramel corn had made me hungry!

That's when a chant broke out. "School fair! School fair! School fair! School fair!"

"Okay, everyone," Ms. Gaffey said. "Let's take it down a notch. I know you're all very excited about the fair coming, but we still have a few more days until it arrives. Let's try to save our excitement until the big day has come, all right?"

The whole class settled down.

That is, until the crackle of the loudspeaker echoed in the classroom and Principal Roberta said, "Nottingham Elementary! Who's ready for the fair on Wednesday?"

That made every kid go, "Woop woop!" and "Ahhhh!" and make all kinds of loud, crazy noises.

Ms. Gaffey shook her head. "Well, I tried," she said quietly.

By the time lunch hit, all anybody could talk about was the fair. Even Ms. Gaffey had given in. "When you return from recess, we'll learn about the history of carnival games and rank our favorite ones," she said.

In the hallway, Sammy swung past me and stopped dead in front. "Are you going to try and dunk Principal Roberta this year?"

I shook my head. Even though the kid who sank the principal

was pretty much the coolest kid in school for weeks on end, I wasn't really interested. I'd always liked Principal Roberta. Plus last week, when she got back from a conference and all my friends told her I didn't deserve the in-school suspension Assistant Principal Johnson had given me, she believed them over him. That made me like her even more.

LJ appeared next to me. "Really? You don't want all the glory of being the person who dunked the principal?"

"Nah," I said. "That's not my style."

"Sure," LJ said. She elbowed Sammy, and they both laughed.

I didn't understand what was so funny.

"Anyway, do you want to take the bus to my house on Wednesday?" LJ asked. "We can hang out, and then my Dad can drive us to the fair."

"Ummmm...," I mumbled. "Maybe."

It wasn't anything against LJ. I definitely wanted to hang out with her at the fair. But for the past few years, I had always gone with Mary Ann.

Because Mary Ann lives right down the street from our school, we were always able to get to the fair early and scope out the best games and the crunchiest, most mouthwatering snacks.

When I thought of the fair, I was just as excited to think about going with Mary Ann as I was about the actual fair. Now that Mary Ann and I were friends again, I really hoped she'd ask me to her house and we'd have all that fun again.

LJ's eyebrows pushed together and she crossed her arms. "Oh, okay," she said.

For some reason, I felt a little uncomfortable, so I put my hood up. Then I walked toward the cafeteria.

But on my way there, I couldn't help but hear all the kids loud-whispering around me.

Why do kids even pretend to whisper when they're being so loud? Like, just talk normal.

Anyway, I slowed down to walk past a bunch of fifth graders who were actually being quiet with their whispers.

It wasn't until I walked past the last two kids that I could really hear what they were saying.

"Did you hear about what Jessie told Elizabeth that Nadia told her?"

"No, what?"

"She's looking for someone to share the reign of the playground."

"Elizabeth said that?"

"No, Nadia said that to Jessie, who told Elizabeth."

"Oooooooh! Get out!"

Honestly, I tried to ignore it for two reasons.

One, anything that had to do

with Nadia and sharing was just Nadia trying to trick kids into some kind of trap. I'd learned that last week, so I wasn't buying it.

And two, my black bean burger and sweet potato fries had been sitting in my lunch box for far too long. I was ready to devour them, and nothing was going to keep me from that.

In the cafeteria, I saw Mary Ann and ran toward her. Jenny was sitting next to her and waved to me.

The very second I sat down, Mary Ann said, "I taught Jenny our old lunch tradition. Do you mind if she joins in?"

I smiled and put my hood back down. "That depends," I said and looked at Jenny. "What do you have for lunch?"

"A ham and cheese sandwich with apple slices," she said.

"Mmmm. Yes, that sounds perfect."

"Let's do fifths," Mary Ann said. "So that we still keep most of our own food."

"Deal," Jenny and I both said.

Okay, I should explain this. When Mary Ann and I were best friends and we sat together at lunch, we had this tradition where we'd cut our food into four equal parts. Then we'd swap one of the fourths with the other person. That way, we got to eat all kinds of different foods for lunch every day.

I took out my plastic knife from the utensil set I always carried and looked at my burger. What was the best way to cut a burger into fifths? I had no idea.

I took the easy way out and separated the fries into five piles first.

LJ sat down in the seat next to me. Then Sammy sat next to her, Allana and Dale sat across the table, and they all started talking to each other.

Once my fries were counted out, I tried to ignore everybody's voices. It wasn't anything against them, it's just that I really wanted to start eating. And even though I'd been getting better at math, cutting a burger into five parts was just totally stumping me.

"Hey, Robin," LJ said. "What do you think about the Nadia rumors? Do you think she's serious about sharing her reign?"

I tugged on the strings of my hood and tried to concentrate on my burger. I thought that maybe if I pulled myself farther into my hoodie, I'd be able to block out all the distractions and figure out how to do this math. I drew out a peace symbol, but that only had four parts.

"Robin?" LJ said.

My stomach gurgled so loudly that I thought it might jump up onto the table and take the whole burger for itself if I didn't start eating in the next few seconds.

So I turned my back to LJ and said, "Hold on, I have to do this first."

I closed my eyes and pretended to cut the burger in my head. I tried four different ways before I realized the right way to do it. I opened my eyes, cut my burger, passed Jenny and Mary Ann their parts, and took one-fifth of their sandwiches, apple slices, and carrot sticks. Then I shoved two apple slices into my mouth, swallowed, turned to LJ, and said, "Okay."

But LJ wasn't there. She'd moved to sit between Sammy and Allana.

I wondered if LJ was mad at me because I hadn't answered her question while I was trying to do fractions. But my wonder only lasted for a second. Even though my stomach was trying, it couldn't eat this lunch on its own! I turned back to Mary Ann and Jenny and chomped down on my food.

After lunch, the whole group and I walked out to the playground. It was super weird out there. Not one kid was playing a game. Nadia stood at the top of the jungle gym, smiling and looking down. Everyone was gathered around her.

I seemed to be the only person who remembered what had happened last week.

I knew that anything Nadia came up with was bogus. If the rumors were true, she was probably going to tell everyone she'd "share her reign" (whatever that even meant), and then, after a kid got their hopes up and jumped through whatever hoops Nadia created, she'd announce that there was never a prize, and the whole thing was some big tricky way to laugh at the kid.

That's exactly what she'd done to me.

After I won her basketball tournament, where she promised to give away half of the Bonus Bucks she'd stolen from kids, she did this:

Okay, it didn't go exactly like that. But it was close.

"So what do you think she means by *share her reign*?" Sammy asked.

Allana and Dale nodded their heads at one another, and Allana started the rap.

Nadia said
She'd share her reign
But figuring that out
Has been a real pain
Some kids think
She's talking about bucks
Other kids say
She's lining up her ducks
Because next year

She's in sixth grade

So they think she's deciding

Who's next to get paid

This year

They'll learn the ropes

And next year

They'll give out cantaloupes.

Allana looked at Dale.

"Hey, they could," he said. Allana rolled her eyes, and he just laughed.

"So you think she's trying to find someone to take over the playground?" Jenny asked.

"That's one rumor," Allana said.

"And then the other one is about bucks?" Sammy asked.

Dale nodded. "Someone said she can't figure out how to charge bucks after getting in trouble. So she wants another person to help come up with a new way, and then they'll get half the bucks."

"I don't know," LJ said. "I think this last detention changed her."

I rolled my eyes. "Yeah right. So you don't think any of the rumors are true?"

"I'm just saying that I don't know what's true." LJ was starting to look angry. But that confused me, because we were talking about Nadia. What was there to be upset about?

I turned to Mary Ann. "What do you think?"

Mary Ann shrugged. "I don't know, either. But I'm excited to eat all the cotton candy I can at the fair on Wednesday."

I smiled. "That is *definitely* something to look forward to."

And then another weird thing happened.

Well, this time it didn't seem all that weird. I was starting to get used to it.

LJ looked at me like I was *made of* cotton candy and I was floating away or something.

"What?" I said.

"You know, people change," LJ said.

"Yeah," I said. "But not Nadia."

And then LJ turned around, but I still heard what she said.

She said, "I didn't say Nadia."

I didn't know what that was supposed to mean, but I did know that I was really ready for some cotton candy.

Also, if I really thought about it, LJ also seemed to be changing.

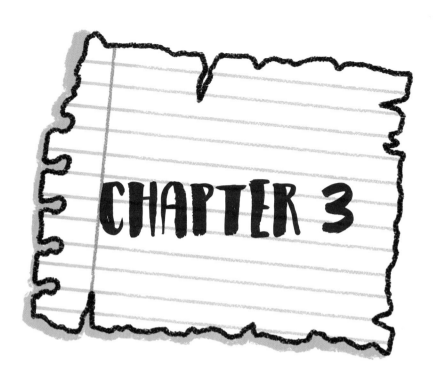

CHAPTER 3

TUESDAY, OCTOBER 8

Last time, when things ended weird with LJ on Saturday, I saw her in school on Monday and it was like nothing had even happened.

I figured it would be the same

way this time. I thought I'd walk into class, and LJ would smile again, and then she'd say something like:

But yeah, LJ didn't say anything like that.

Because she didn't say anything to me at all.

Not when I walked over to my desk and smiled at her.

Not when I said, "Hey LJ," as I took the books out of my backpack.

Not even when I thought she maybe didn't hear me, so I said, "LJ, hey, I said hi," and waved my hand in front of her face.

That's when she turned to Allana and said, "What do you and Dale have planned for the morning rap today?"

It's also when my face turned

bright red like an apple. I put my hood up and sat down in my seat.

Obviously, LJ was acting like she was mad at me or something, but she wasn't telling me why.

I hadn't had a friend in this class for a whole month before I met LJ, so I really didn't mind not talking to her now. It gave me time to think about why I was actually a little bit mad at her, too.

When LJ and I had played in the basketball tournament last week, we'd been a team. She was just as mad as I was when Nadia yelled that she wasn't going to share her bucks after I'd won her trick competition.

Yet here we were, only like eleven days later, and LJ was pretending that the whole thing hadn't happened.

I looked over at Nadia. She saw me looking at her and stuck her tongue out.

I narrowed my eyes and turned back toward the blackboard. Why would anyone think Nadia had changed? Clearly, she was just as mean as ever.

And it wasn't very best-friend-like of LJ to just pretend we didn't have that history with Nadia. Or to ignore me.

So when LJ didn't say one word, even when she had to pass a grammar test forward, or hand me her math homework from last night, I joined in the silence.

Thankfully, I still had other friends who wanted to talk to me. And not about Nadia!

When class was over, I walked down the hall with the twins and Sammy, stopping at my locker to grab my lunch.

"Robin, settle a bet for us," Dale said. "Which one of us do you think can shove more caramel corn in their face, me or Allana?"

"Allana. Sorry, Dale," I said.

Allana pumped her fist in the air. Dale sighed and shook his head.

"You'll see," Dale said. "You'll all see."

"You're both going to get stomachaches," Sammy said.

"Hopefully!" Allana said, and she laughed.

Then a tap on my shoulder made me pause.

I thought maybe it was LJ. I took a deep breath, ready to turn around and hear her apology.

I was ready for her to say, "You know what, you're right. Nadia hasn't changed, and I should have realized that."

But . . . yeah. I didn't need to be ready for that.

Because it was Mary Ann and Jenny.

"I meant to ask you this yesterday," Mary Ann said as we walked into the cafeteria. "Do you want to come over to my house after school tomorrow? That way we can all go to the fair together."

"Just like we used to!" I was so happy. Mary Ann *had* remembered our tradition! "Can we go a little early and scope out all the yummy food again?"

"You know it," Mary Ann said. "Jenny, we'll show you around. I bet they put the candy apples next to the fishbowl game again!"

"They do it every year," I said as I sat down at our table. "And it stinks because I get so close to getting the ring into the fishbowl, and then I see those candy apples out of the corner of my eye. It totally breaks my concentration!"

As soon as I sat down, I started dividing my lunch into fifths so I could share with Mary Ann and Jenny again. After conquering that fraction yesterday, it was easy.

"Allana, Dale, and Sammy," Mary Ann said. "Would you like to come to my house after school tomorrow and go to the fair early? My mom has a minivan, so she can give you all rides home afterward."

At first, I thought Mary Ann didn't ask LJ because she somehow knew that I was mad at LJ and that LJ was mad at me. But it felt mean to ask everyone else in front of LJ and leave her out.

But when I looked up, I saw that LJ wasn't at the lunch table.

"We have to ask Dad and Pop," Allana said. "But..." She looked at

Dale, who nodded his head. "We'd love to."

"Great!" Mary Ann said. "Sammy, what about you?"

Sammy bit the inside of his cheek. He whispered, "I'm going with LJ."

"Where *is* LJ?" I asked.

Dale and Allana looked at one another and nodded.

She told us she
had to talk to someone
And then she bolted
Just up and gone!

I looked around the cafeteria. Who could LJ be talking to? All of her friends were at this lunch table. Did she have a kid sister I was forgetting about? No, LJ was the youngest of her family. Did she have friends from last year that she just never mentioned?

The ideas rolled around in my head like peas on a plate.

Until I just stopped.

I was mad at LJ, so she could go talk to whoever she wanted, and I didn't need to know who it was. It's not like she was going to tell me, anyway!

It wasn't until the lunch bell

rang and I went to throw away my garbage that I saw something out of the corner of my eye.

And it wasn't a candy apple. *Man, I could really go for one of those right now.*

But it *was* as distracting as those candy apples.

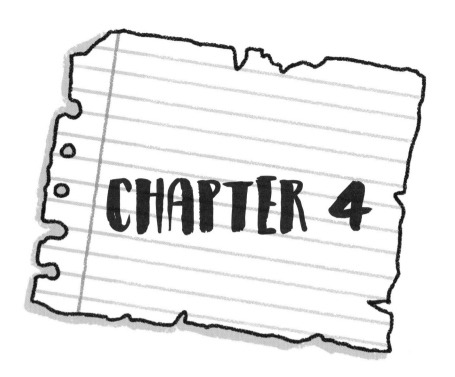

CHAPTER 4

"You guys are *not* going to believe what I just saw!" I yelled as soon as we got outside.

Everyone froze and spun around to look at me.

"What?" Jenny asked.

"LJ and *Nadia*," I said, pausing

to really let it sink in. "Eating lunch together! And talking!"

Mary Ann put her hand over her mouth. She understood what a big deal this was.

But Sammy, Allana, and Dale didn't say anything. They all just gave each other quick little looks.

"Do you guys know something?" I asked.

But before Sammy could say anything, I heard a pair of loud laughs that I knew all too well.

I turned around and saw Nadia and LJ walking to the playground. Something was going on. It was all pretty clear to me.

Nadia waved to LJ and headed to the jungle gym. LJ walked toward us.

I felt like I'd swallowed a whole bottle of hot sauce and my body had turned into that bottle. I couldn't breathe, but I was also breathing too fast. I pulled on the strings of my hoodie, and the second LJ walked into the circle, I yelled, "Why were you with *Nadia,* of all people?"

LJ rolled her eyes. She crossed her arms and straightened her back. At first she didn't answer, but then Mary Ann asked, "Were you trying to figure out what's going on?"

LJ nodded. "There are all these rumors going around, and I wanted to know if any of them were true."

"But why do you even care?" I asked.

"Why *don't* you care?" LJ stood directly in front of me. She looked down at me, which was kind of easy for her because she is SO tall. "Last week we were all about trying to beat Nadia at her own game to help the kids on this playground. Maybe I'm still trying to do that."

I didn't buy it. If that was

what LJ was trying to do, why wouldn't she have talked to me about it first? We'd taken on Nadia *together* last time. Plus yesterday, LJ thought Nadia had changed. Why would she be "beating" Nadia if she thought Nadia was actually a nice person now?

I may have been mad at LJ, but I needed her to see what was going on.

"But don't you realize that she's *not* going to let you win? She always has a dirty trick up her sleeve. It's obvious this is just another mean scheme."

LJ huffed. "She doesn't *always*

have a dirty trick up her sleeve. She was mad at YOU, if you remember, and wanted to get back at you. That's why she was nasty about the basketball tournament."

That hurt.

It hurt because it was true. Nadia had been trying to get back at me because I'd accidentally busted her cousin's nose with a basketball.

But she was also mad about all her Bonus Bucks being stolen. And even though Nadia didn't know it, LJ and I had stolen them together.

For LJ to make it sound like

it was just me . . . well, that felt mean.

"So what are you trying to do?" I asked. "Win some made-up Help the Playground Award?"

But LJ ignored my question.

"Nadia's offering to share her reign of the playground. I did find out what game you have to win. She's going to have a Skee-Ball tournament at the fair," LJ said. Then she mumbled, "Plus she told me some other stuff."

I rolled my eyes so hard I thought they were going to turn into hardboiled eggs and roll right across the playground.

"What other stuff?" I asked.

"It doesn't matter," LJ said. "The game is what's important."

"So, what you're really saying is that she didn't tell you anything. And you still think she's not just playing a trick on everyone?"

LJ crossed her arms. "I think it's worth at least trying to win her tournament."

"Well, I think that's silly. What do you guys think?" I turned to everyone else.

Allana and Dale looked at one another and frowned. They rapped their response like this:

"Sammy?" I asked.

"I . . ." he mumbled so softly you'd think his mouth was full of marshmallows and he couldn't get out the words. "I . . . don't make me say it."

LJ put her hand on Sammy's shoulder, and Sammy's cheeks turned pink like a shrimp's tail. She turned to me and said, "Whatever happened to doing what's right for the playground? Whatever happened to trying to make things better?"

"How is taking half of Nadia's bucks helping?"

LJ's eyes widened, and she took a step back.

"Wow," she said. "I can't believe you think I'd take her bucks, not that she's even taxing anymore. You really don't get it."

LJ turned around and walked away.

"LJ," I said. "Come back."

She did turn back, but only to say, "I really thought I knew you, but I guess not." Then she walked across the playground toward the jungle gym.

I threw my hands in the air. "Can you believe this?" I said.

Sammy, Allana, and Dale didn't say anything.

But Mary Ann did. "I don't think LJ realizes how mad Nadia was about that detention. Principal Roberta had me leave the room while she talked to Nadia about her punishment, but I saw Nadia's face when she left."

I had totally forgotten that Mary Ann knew firsthand how upset Nadia had been because she was part of the reason Principal Roberta had punished Nadia. Mary Ann had told the principal how it was all Nadia's fault that I had in-school suspension. Then Mary Ann had used her Principal for the Day badge to remove my suspension and give Principal Roberta all sorts of ideas about stuff Nadia should be punished for.

"She may have gotten rid of taxing for now, but I think you're right, Robin," Mary Ann said. "I think Nadia's just looking for another way to make us pay."

Jenny nodded her head. "And there's no way she'd share her rule of the playground with someone else."

"Yup," Mary Ann said. "She's probably just trying to find someone to do her dirty work for her."

"You're right," I said. "And LJ doesn't even see it."

I looked over at the jungle gym. Nadia had slid down the slide and was sitting at the bottom, talking to LJ.

Now, instead of being mad at LJ, I just felt bad for her. It was so clear that Nadia was going to take advantage of her, and LJ just wanted to see the good in Nadia.

How could I get LJ to see that not everyone was as good as she wanted to believe?

CHAPTER 5

WEDNESDAY, OCTOBER 9

Yesterday on the playground was the last time LJ and I spoke.

One part of me is angry at LJ for making it sound like everything with Nadia was all my fault.

But the other part of me is sad.

I'm like one of those string cheeses that's half cheddar, half mozzarella. The kind you split in two so you can eat both cheeses separately.

LJ hadn't talked to me at all about trying to win back the playground. I had just met her when I asked her to help me defeat Nadia. It was taking down Nadia that had made us such close friends, but now she wasn't including me.

I know that I joked about my nickname being The Outlaw, but really, I thought of that as the name for me *and* LJ. And now, it felt like LJ was trying to be The Outlaw all on her own.

Usually when my angry feelings and my sad feelings combine, it makes me extra angry.

But this time, I felt them split into two very different parts of me and, well...it made me quiet.

I tried talking to LJ yesterday, but all the angry parts spilled out.

Because of that, I didn't think she'd want to hear any of the sad stuff.

All I could do was hope that after she lost the competition, she'd come back to me, apologizing for not including me. Or that if she did win, she'd see Nadia pull the rug out from under her. Maybe Nadia would announce that LJ was really going to be her number fifteen, not her number two. Then maybe LJ would realize that I was trying to look out for her this whole time. That I was just trying to do what was right, like I always do. She'd say she was sorry, and then everything could go back to the way it was.

For now, we just sat in silence and avoided looking at each other while we listened to Ms. Gaffey and waited for lunch to come around.

In fact, with all my emotions pulling me in different directions, I'd almost forgotten that the fair was after school today!

It wasn't until I walked into the cafeteria and saw all the kids lined up against the windows that I remembered.

I walked over to stand next to Mary Ann and smushed my face against the glass. You could see some adults assembling the stands for the games.

"All right, kids," Ms. Gaffey said. (It was her day to watch us during lunch.) "Let's get back to the tables."

As I pulled away from the window, I turned toward Mary Ann, who was turned toward Jenny and talking to her.

"Let's show Robin the dance we made up last month, in case we hear the same song playing at the fair," Mary Ann said to Jenny.

"The one by Renaissance that's always on the radio?" Jenny smiled. "Yes! Maybe Allana and Dale would sing it for us."

"We can definitely do that," Allana said.

"Just give us a beat!" Dale added.

"I'm so glad everyone can come over," Mary Ann said. "My mom said we can all hang out for a little bit before we go to the fair."

"Could we maybe just drop off our backpacks and then go right to the fair early?" I asked. That had been our tradition for as long as I could remember. I hoped

Mary Ann wouldn't stop doing that now. "After we learn the dance, I guess."

Mary Ann looked at the other kids in the group, but everyone was shaking their heads no.

She shrugged her shoulders. "Maybe."

When we sat down, Sammy was already at the table, moping over his macaroni and cheese.

"What's wrong?" Jenny asked.

"LJ's not sitting with us."

"So?" I said, separating my grapes, cheese slices, and crackers into five piles. "She's probably sitting with her new best friend, Nadia."

Sammy sighed. "I miss her."

"It's been one day," I mumbled under my breath, but I knew I was loud enough for everyone to hear me.

Sammy surprised me. He said, "Yeah! And I *still* miss her! Don't you?"

I shrugged. Then, I put my hood up.

I did miss LJ. But I still had all kinds of mixed feelings about how things were with her. One day wasn't enough time for me to be *that* upset that she wasn't at the lunch table.

Besides, today was the fair!

Which meant LJ would do the competition, Nadia would reveal that she was still just a big meanie, LJ would decide to come back for tomorrow's lunch, and hopefully everything would be fine again.

Sammy got up. "I'm going to find her."

Allana and Dale nodded to one another.

Sammy and LJ
Sitting in a tree
K-I-S-S-
I-N-G
First comes love
Then comes marriage

Then comes puppies

Cuz not everyone wants kids.

"True story," Dale said. "I had to sacrifice the rhyme for the truth. Our Aunt Dotty tells us she's never having kids. But she's got three dogs, and they're awesome."

Everybody laughed and nodded their heads.

Except Sammy. He started breathing really quickly and picked up his lunch tray. "LJ's one of my best friends, that's all," he said. Then he turned around and left the table.

CHAPTER 6

The walk to Mary Ann's house was crazy.

First, half of the booths were completely set up. Kids were weaving their way through the stands to see what there was to play and eat this year.

I like to watch as much of the fair get put together as I can. Then, once every last bolt has been screwed in and every last prize has been hung, I like to slowly walk through, making a mental list of every food, how much it costs, and what games I would actually sacrifice food money for.

Some kids are in it for the prizes, but not me. I like the thrill of the game!

Another reason that the trip to Mary Ann's was nuts was because there were more kids walking home today than getting on buses. I guess there are a bunch of other kids who live near the school, too. And all of them had the same idea as Mary Ann.

Allana, Dale, Jenny, Mary Ann, and I all walked together toward Mary Ann's house.

I walked backward as slowly as possible, so I could see all the parents, volunteers, and fair workers putting everything together. I was also hoping my friends would slow down and wait for me.

But when I turned my head in the direction I was moving, everyone was running toward Mary Ann's house.

So that plan was out the window.

Once we got to Mary Ann's house, we all put our backpacks in her living room and then watched a show about turtles.

Well, everyone else watched it. I tapped my foot and daydreamed about candy apples as big as my head. I wanted to skedaddle!

After the show was over, we headed to the front lawn. Jenny and Mary Ann kept trying to show me their dance moves, but the second I landed in Mary Ann's house, any hope of me learning a dance was gone. I was way too distracted thinking about the fair.

So I didn't really pick up the moves too well.

They danced around me in circles for what felt like forever.

I think it was really about ten minutes.

"Robin, you're not even trying," Mary Ann said.

"I just…" I shook my head. "I just really want to go to the fair."

Allana looked at her watch. "We still have fifteen minutes until it starts."

"There's only fifteen minutes?!" I yelled. "Please, can we go now?"

Mary Ann laughed and shook her head. "Let me go ask my mom."

Thankfully, Mary Ann's mom said yes, and we all headed to the fair.

The rest of the group walked. I ran as fast as my legs would take me.

When I got close, I had to stop.

It looked like something out of a fairy tale!

As we walked into the tent, I felt all my cares and worries disappear.

We walked past the ring toss game where you can win a goldfish, which was next to the candy apples. Mary Ann said, "I told you! I told you!" as we passed. My stomach growled as I walked by the funnel cake stand.

Funnel cake. How could I have forgotten the best fair food of them all?

I only had $10 to spend, so I had to spend it wisely.

Allana and Dale beelined across the fair and we all ran to catch up. They'd spotted the caramel corn stand.

"Two bags, please!" Allana said.

"I can't serve anything until the fair starts," the woman inside the booth said. "Come back in five minutes."

"Pleeeeaaassse," Allana and Dale said in unison.

The woman laughed. "Oh, all right. I guess it's fine."

She handed them each a bag of caramel corn. "Now don't eat it all at once," she said.

"Oh, but we will!" Dale said. He and Allana turned and walked back toward the rest of our group.

"How are you going to tell who has more popcorn in their mouth?" I asked.

"We're going to dump the bags into our mouths and see whose bag has less popcorn left in it," Allana said.

I couldn't disagree with their logic.

I also couldn't help but laugh as the twins counted down from five to one, closed their eyes, and then turned the bags upside down.

I started to ask, "So, are you going to put the stuff on the ground back into the bags, or what?"

But the twins couldn't hear me because they were still trying to pour more and more caramel corn into their mouths.

Two seconds into the fair and they were already making a mess!

They both opened their eyes and looked at their empty bags of corn.

"M m n z z mmpfee," Allana said, mouth stuffed.

"Shh iff mmnn," Dale said.

"You shouldn't talk with your mouth full," said a familiar voice.

I turned around and saw Sammy standing behind me.

"Oh, hey," I said. I looked around. "I thought you were coming with LJ."

Sammy nodded. "She's over there getting a head start on the Skee-Ball competition." He pointed behind us.

I turned around. Technically, the fair wouldn't begin for another couple of minutes, but there was already a small group of kids playing Skee-Ball.

Apparently, the Skee-Ball worker was pretty lax about starting the fair on time! Then again, so was the caramel corn woman.

There were only six machines,

but every single one was being used.

All of those uncomfortable feelings that had disappeared when I walked into the fair came rushing back to me when I saw Nadia like this:

But I couldn't have heard that right.

I expected Nadia to say, "BOOOOO!" to LJ. I expected her to stop pretending to be nice. Now that the tournament was actually happening, I thought Nadia would be mean to LJ.

But...yeah. Nadia was actually rooting for LJ!

I had to do something to distract myself. This fair was one of my favorite things all year. It was time to enjoy it!

"Well, we can have our own fun!" I said.

"Yrrf!" Allana and Dale said.

"What game should we try first?" Mary Ann asked.

"Oooh! Oooh!" Jenny said. "Can we please get our faces painted before the line gets long?"

"That's a great idea!" Mary Ann said. "What do you guys think?"

Allana and Dale excitedly nodded their heads.

Sammy looked back over at the Skee-Ball. "I'm going to cheer LJ on. But I'll see you guys later."

I wasn't a big fan of getting my face painted, plus the stand was directly across from Skee-Ball. But then I realized that standing there would let me keep an eye on Nadia.

Anyway, thanks to my really good group of friends and the awesomeness of the fair, we had some great times over the next hour or two:

I ended up winning enough goldfish to give one to each of my friends.

Allana and Dale even rapped about it.

Robin is the
    Ring toss queen
She's the best fair winner
    Of all the preteens

"Guys, please, I just have a knack for this game," I said. My cheeks felt like they were as red as a candy apple. And oh man— I really needed to get one of those before they ran out!

I put my hood up and pulled on the strings. "The trick is to pretend like it's a basketball hoop and you're trying to get it straight through."

Behind me, I heard cheering and hooting and hollering. For a second, I thought that maybe, because my friends had been cheering me on during the goldfish game, there might be a crowd of kids around.

But...well. There *was* a whole ruckus going on. But it wasn't for me.

It was for LJ.

Every kid from our school was crowded around the Skee-Ball machines. I pushed my way through, looking for Sammy. He was in the front row, making the most noise of anyone.

LJ was playing against two kids. One of them was Aaron, Nadia's cousin. The other was a second grader named Shawn. It was anybody's game until Shawn tossed the Skee-Ball up the ramp and it didn't land in any of the holes. Meanwhile, Aaron and LJ both scored in the 100-point rings. Then the buzzer went off.

"Good try, Shawn," Nadia said. She patted Shawn on the shoulder. Then she turned to LJ and Aaron. "All right, for this last match, I want you to switch machines," she told them.

Aaron looked mad. "Why?" he said.

"Because I said so," Nadia said.

LJ didn't look like she cared either way.

But I knew immediately why Nadia would do something like that. She must have noticed that the machine Aaron was playing on was busted, so it was harder to get points. Yeah, Aaron had been doing well anyway, but he'd been playing on the broken machine this whole time. He was used to it and had figured out how to do well on it.

LJ wouldn't have a clue, and she'd do really bad. Nadia's cousin would win, and it would make LJ look terrible.

I thought about telling LJ, but I decided against it. She hadn't believed anything else I'd said to her about Nadia. Why would she believe this?

The buzzer went off, and Aaron and LJ started the next game.

The crowd cheered them on. Nadia stood next to LJ and watched the scoreboard. I did, too.

LJ rolled a ball, and it went into the ten-point ring.

I waited for the scoreboard not to light up. I waited for her to realize that this one was rigged, and she'd only be able to score in the harder rings.

But something way more unexpected happened! When the ball went into the hole, her score went up by twenty points!

I blinked a whole bunch of times. I had to be seeing it wrong.

LJ rolled a second ball and it

went in the fifty-point ring, and her score went up by fifty.

I figured, *Okay, I* am *seeing things wrong.*

But then she rolled another ball into the ten-point ring, and her score went up by twenty again!

The machine wasn't rigged to lose. It was rigged to *win*!

My mind exploded like a bag of popcorn that had been ripped open.

How could this be? Why would Nadia switch Aaron and LJ like that? I tried to put the pieces together, but nothing made sense.

The buzzer went off, and LJ had beaten Aaron by over fifty points.

Nadia took LJ's hand and raised it in the air. She said, "I hereby declare LJ the winner!"

Then I waited for her to say something like, "But now you're going to be sorry, because you're actually going to do all of my homework for the rest of the year." Or, "But this whole contest didn't mean anything. There is no winner!"

But...I couldn't catch a break. Nothing was going the way I thought it would, because the next thing Nadia said was, "And that makes her the new co-queen of the playground!"

And then...

My eyes were stinging like I'd gotten pepper in them. I rubbed them hard, and I looked again. I couldn't believe it. Nadia was being nice to LJ.

Too nice, if you asked me.

And then, just as I was trying to understand what had just happened, my stomach flipped right over on me.

I walked over to the twins. They looked pretty rough, too. Their faces were as green as cucumbers. Allana nodded at Dale and Dale clutched his stomach.

Turns out eating
So much food
Was a bad idea
We had no clue!
Our stomachs are full
This must be a fluke

Then Dale ran toward a trash can. I had to look away. I always puked when I saw someone else puke.

My stomach was making scary noises, Dale was sick, and Nadia was still tricking LJ, even though I couldn't figure out how.

Wednesday was officially the new worst day ever.

Especially after Dale puked again.

And then I puked.

CHAPTER 7

THURSDAY, OCTOBER 10

The fair had been totally ruined for me.

And not just because of all the puking.

It was mostly because of what

had happened between LJ and Nadia.

I'd tried talking it through with Sammy, but he'd just said, "Maybe LJ was right. Maybe Nadia has really changed."

But he obviously wasn't thinking clearly.

I didn't get a chance to talk about it with Dale and Allana last night. Their Dad and Pop had picked them up early from the fair because they weren't feeling too well.

Mary Ann and Jenny didn't even seem to understand why I was upset.

"I don't know," Mary Ann had said as we'd walked back to her house. "It was just a game."

But I didn't believe that. I didn't believe what any of them said. It couldn't be that simple.

So my worry now was that Nadia must have still been really angry at me for getting her in so much trouble. She must be using LJ to get back at me.

Now *that* made sense.

If she could steal LJ by tricking her into this competition and pretending to be a nice person, then she could tell LJ all kinds of mean things about me. Maybe even turn LJ against me.

That had to be it!

But now the question was, how could I get LJ back? On the bus ride to school today, it was all I could think about.

Usually, I spend the bus ride still thinking about breakfast and when I'd get to eat lunch. But this Nadia and LJ stuff was really throwing me off.

It practically spun me for a loop when I walked into the classroom and saw this:

Okay, no. I didn't really do that. I didn't go THAT bananas.

But in my head, I did. In my head, I was shooting off into the sky.

In reality, I played it really cool and said, "Please get out of my seat, Nadia."

Nadia and LJ looked at me like I'd grown Twizzlers in place of my hair, and they were also afraid of Twizzlers. I put my hood up.

"I was just talking to LJ," Nadia said. "Besides, you weren't here yet."

I walked over to my desk and crossed my arms. I tapped my foot on the ground.

"Well, I'm here now," I said. "So please go to your own seat."

Nadia rolled her eyes and stood up. "I'll see you at lunch, LJ."

LJ smiled at Nadia, and Nadia went back to her own seat.

"At lunch?" Sammy asked loudly.

I threw my backpack down and crashed into my seat. I pulled on the strings of my hoodie. I wanted to sink away from everyone.

"Did you hear that I won Nadia's competition yesterday?" LJ asked me.

I guess LJ was taking punches at me every day now.

I didn't turn around. It hurt that she hadn't even seen me yesterday. I'd been in the front row, right next to Sammy.

Or she was just rubbing it in. Either way, it wasn't nice.

"And after that," she continued, "I dunked Principal Roberta in the dunk tank."

"Whatever," I said.

"You could be happy for me," LJ said.

I turned around. I still felt kind of bad for LJ. She couldn't see what was happening. None of them could. I was the only one, and no one would listen to me.

"You still don't get it," I said. "This is just some long game on Nadia's end. You'll see."

I waited for LJ to say something snippy back. I also thought there was a small chance she'd whisper, "You're probably right."

But ... nothing happened. She didn't say anything at all.

So I just sat at my desk, my hood pressed against my face and my thoughts all swirly and tight in my head.

They stayed that way, even when Ms. Gaffey passed out our math test. The way my head was all filled with angry thoughts made it hard to focus. Lately I'd been checking my answers twice, but I didn't do that this time. There were some questions I skipped altogether.

All I could think was that I just wanted Nadia to reveal her big evil plan so LJ and I could go back to being friends, and then this would all be over with.

When the lunch bell rang, I loosened my hood and put it back down. I needed something good to happen. And I knew just who could help.

I turned to the twins as we walked down the hall.

"Allana, Dale, will you two rap about something funny for me? I could use a pick-me-up."

But my funniest friends weren't feeling too hot themselves.

Dale had his hand on his stomach, and his face still looked pretty green.

Allana had her hand on his back when she turned to me. "I'm sorry,

Robin. I don't think Dale can do it today. He really doesn't feel well. Our dads were upset that Dale made himself sick, so they made Dale come to school anyway."

Even though it should have been a not-great moment, it went like this for me:

I'm not sure why, but something about what Allana said made all the gears in my head start turning.

Dale's dads were mad at Dale for eating all that food that made his stomach upset. Dale had done it to himself, even knowing it would end badly.

With LJ, she didn't know that what she was doing was going to end in disaster, so she couldn't help but make the wrong choice. But that wasn't her fault. It was mine, for not getting her to understand it better. I was getting madder when I should have been getting smarter.

Maybe I needed to think more like Nadia.

I sat down next to Sammy at the lunch table.

"She'll be back tomorrow, huh?" Sammy said.

"I know, I know," I said. "I should have tried harder to talk her out of that competition! But it's too late for that now. Now we need to get her back!"

Dale had his head propped up on the table with his hand. "I don't know. She seems to like Nadia." He pointed in their direction. "Look at them."

We looked over and saw Nadia,

LJ, Aaron, and Ty all talking and laughing together. A couple of kids walked by and tapped LJ on the back. She turned around, and they said, "Wow, you dunked Principal Roberta! That's so cool!" LJ blushed.

Nadia stood up. "Give the girl some space, she's trying to eat lunch."

The kids all high-fived LJ and then walked away.

I shook my head. "Obviously Nadia has her under some kind of spell."

"I don't think Nadia does magic," Sammy said.

"No, I mean she's tricking LJ.

Nadia's making LJ think that everything in her world is perfect and awesome and that she's some really good person, when we all know that's not true."

"You think so?" Allana said.

"I know so," I said. "We just need to get LJ to come back. We need to steal her back, just like Nadia stole her from us."

Someone cleared their throat really loudly, and it startled me so much I almost flipped my entire tray over.

I looked to where the sound had come from and realized Mary Ann was sitting across from me. I didn't know if she'd just sat down and was having a bad day or if she'd been sitting there and I just hadn't noticed.

"So...are we sharing our lunches today?" Mary Ann asked me.

Seemed like it was definitely the last one.

But I had bigger things to worry about. "Can we wait on that? I need to come up with a plan to steal LJ back."

Mary Ann looked sad for a couple of seconds, but then she blinked a lot, smiled, and whispered something to Jenny.

Allana stared at her food. "What

if LJ really did want to help the playground? And she's pretending to be friends with Nadia because she really does want to do what's best for the rest of the kids."

"I don't know," I said. I looked over at the two of them. Even though LJ was sitting next to Nadia and they were talking like two regular kids, I imagined it looked more like this:

"If that's true," Allana said, "then what if we announced a big contest to take over the playground during recess? LJ would see that we want to take over from Nadia. She'd try out, and we'd let her win! That way, we don't have to steal her. We can just kind of make up our own contest."

Dale looked up from the table at Allana. I could hear him whisper, "I thought we were staying out of it."

Allana shrugged and whispered back, "LJ doesn't hang out with us anymore. I miss her."

"Why don't you just ask her to sit with us again?" Mary Ann asked.

"That won't work," I said. "Nadia has her tricked really good. We'll have to do something that tricks her into coming back."

I turned to Allana. "I think your plan could work. Let's figure out what it's all going to look like and then announce it at the end of recess. What do you guys think?"

Sammy was the first to speak up. "I'm out," he said. And then he stood up and left the table.

"I'm in," Allana said. She and I high-fived.

Dale put his head on the table and buried it in his arms.

"Dale's in, too," Allana said.

I looked over at Mary Ann and Jenny. "What about you two?" I asked.

Mary Ann looked at me like I'd turned into a bag of yellow onions. She just shook her head and turned to Jenny. Jenny looked at her food and picked little pieces off of it.

"Guess that's a no, then," I said. I turned to Allana and Dale and said, "Okay, let's get to work."

Our new plan was foolproof. Recess was going to be huge!

STILL ONE DAY AFTER THE WORST DAY EVER!

NOT LOOKING MUCH BETTER

CHAPTER 8

So, recess wasn't huge.

It was actually really strange.

When recess started, I looked over at the jungle gym, expecting to see Nadia up on the big slide. But to my surprise, it was empty.

I looked from side to side and

saw that she was on the basketball court, playing with LJ, Aaron, and Ty.

I had to blink fifteen times before I realized that Sammy was also there as the ref.

Allana and Dale stood next to me. I threw my hood up and pulled on the strings so hard that there was only a small circle for me to see through.

Mary Ann came up beside me and pulled on my sleeve.

"Robin, do you want to play jump rope?" she asked.

Well, I think she asked that. I was so busy staring at the court,

I only heard bits and pieces of what she said. I think that's when she pulled on my sleeve a second time. I turned to her and said, "Huh?"

She sighed, but it also sounded like there was food stuck in her throat and she was trying to get it out. "Did you even hear what I said?" she asked.

But I was so mad about the basketball game that I just said, "Yeah," and then turned back. It looked like they were done playing, because Nadia and LJ walked over to the grass with Sammy. The three of them sat down in a circle and laughed.

"They've tricked Sammy now, too!" I said.

But my hood was too tight, so it sounded like I said, "Therrve trkkd thammie nuh, too!"

Now it was Allana's turn to look at me and say, "Huh?"

I loosened my hood and repeated myself.

"Maybe..." Dale began. He took a few deep breaths, wobbled, and then steadied himself. "Maybe Sammy just wants to hang out with LJ."

At least, I think he said that, because that's when I stormed off to the middle of the playground.

Allana ran after me and stood beside me.

"HEY EVERYONE!" I yelled.

I waited for everyone to stop drawing with the sidewalk chalk and playing kickball and four square. I waited for a hush to fall over the playground and everyone to look at me.

But . . . yeah. It didn't go like that at all.

Literally no one stopped doing anything.

I looked around the playground and caught Sammy looking over at me. But then he looked right back at LJ and kept talking.

I started getting really upset. This plan had to work.

"I've got an idea," Allana said. "What if you go to the top of the jungle gym? Then they'll hear you really good."

I nodded my head and ran toward the jungle gym.

"Excuse me," I said as I pushed past a first grader. "You'll thank me once I'm up there."

"Robin!" Allana yelled, but I didn't stop to turn around. I rushed up the stairs. Then I jumped over the edge and stood at the top of the big slide. I closed my eyes and shouted even louder than before.

I didn't even look to see if anyone had heard me that time. I turned around, ran down the stairs, and saw Allana look at me like I had spoken the whole thing in German, and she didn't understand German.

"That's not what we talked

about," she said. "You didn't even mention me or Dale."

"I can tell them those details tomorrow," I said. "Nadia was just as vague when she announced her thing."

"Yeah," Allana said. The bell rang. Recess was over. Then she took Dale's hand and started walking away. "But I didn't think we were trying to do things the way Nadia did."

I didn't know what Allana was talking about. The contest didn't really matter, anyway. The whole point was to just get LJ to be friends with us again.

I saw Mary Ann and Jenny and walked over to them. "Could you hear me from down here?" I asked Mary Ann.

She ignored me and kept walking. I tapped her arm.

"What?" she asked. She didn't turn toward me at all.

"I asked if you—"

"Yeah, sure, whatever," Mary Ann said, hurrying ahead. "Let's go, Jenny."

Why was everyone acting so weird?

I hurried into the school, trying to understand what was going on with my friends.

2 DAYS since the WORST DAY EVER!!
AND IT'S ONLY GETTING WORSE!!
Y
BEST DAY EVER
X
WORST DAY EVER!

CHAPTER 9

FRIDAY, OCTOBER 11

Today, I walked into in Ms. Gaffey's classroom and said, "Hey," to Allana and Dale. Dale smiled the smallest of smiles at me, but Allana was reading and didn't even look up.

The first thing I did after I unpacked my bag was spin around to look at LJ.

"Did you hear my announcement yesterday?"

LJ looked down at her desk. "Mmm."

"Are you going to—" I started to ask.

But Ms. Gaffey interrupted me. "Ms. Loxley, may I see you, please?"

"Yes, Ms. Gaffey," I said.

I stood up and followed her over to her desk.

"Have a seat," she said.

That's when I knew it wasn't

going to be good news. Ms. Gaffey never gave good news sitting down.

"I have your latest math test," she said. She shuffled the papers on her desk and pulled one off the top. She handed it to me.

Normally, when I get a test back, I do this thing where I close my eyes and put the test facedown before I see my grade. Then I squint at it and flip it over really quickly, to see how I did.

But I couldn't do that this time. Ms. Gaffey let go of the paper and I almost caught it, but it slipped and fell into my lap.

My eyes got as big as pancakes.

CHAPTER 10

Lunch today was just absolutely awful.

I sat down at the lunch table and started to eat my ham and cheese sandwich. I waited for Allana, Dale, and Sammy to come. I waited for Mary Ann and Jenny to come. I realized I hadn't cut up my sandwich, so I quickly separated my apple slices into five piles so I could share them.

But...man. Nobody came.

I didn't look around because I just kept hoping one of them would surprise me and say, "Boo! Sorry, Robin. We were all doing an extra-credit project together and ran late."

Well, that seemed unlikely. But I did think they'd come over and talk to me about the contest. Allana had come up with most of it, so I figured she'd come over and want to talk about the details.

But she never came.

No one did.

When I walked out to the playground, I saw kids playing everywhere.

I cleared my throat as loudly as I could. "The contest will begin! Follow me!" I shouted.

Nobody looked at me.

I cleared my throat again.

I walked all the way over to the four square courts, which were on the farthest side of the playground. I took my time, so kids would have a chance to follow me. I walked tall and put my hood up, so everyone would see it and come running over.

But that was the moment I realized my plan wasn't going to work out the way I'd hoped.

A group of second graders walked over to the four square court. A girl in pink shorts dropped a ball, and it rolled toward me.

"Are you here for the contest?" I asked, throwing the ball back to her.

The four kids looked at each other and then at me.

"What contest?" she asked.

It was humiliating enough that I had sat alone at lunch, but this was even worse. I'd come out ready to hold this big contest to win back LJ, and not only did none of my friends come to help, not one kid showed up to compete.

I walked over to the school and leaned against it, then slid down with my back against the wall. I looked around and tried to figure out where everything went wrong.

And then I saw it.

Well, it wasn't an *it*. It was a *her*.

Nadia was in the grass, laughing and pointing at the playground.

She was mocking me, I was sure of it.

I didn't even look to see who she was with. I just stood up and headed right for her.

I was going to let her have it, once and for all.

I ran toward Nadia, and I didn't slow down until I was right behind her. Then I put my hood down and started yelling.

CHAPTER 11

The last two weeks have been some of the toughest I've ever been through, and it's all been because of Nadia. She kept interfering in my life, and I was done with it.

So this time, I really did go bananas.

"Did you tell everyone not to compete?" I yelled. "Did you tell them you'd take away all their bucks or something? Did you make up some really terrible rumors about me, or—"

"Robin, stop it!"

I took a deep breath and looked to my right. LJ was sitting there.

With Mary Ann, Sammy, Allana, and Dale.

"Where's Jenny? She wasn't good enough for you?" I said to Nadia.

"Robin!" Mary Ann said. "She's out sick today. Jeez."

"I didn't do anything," Nadia said. "And I really mean it this time!"

"I don't believe you!" I said.

"Look! You've stolen all my friends! They're all here with you, instead of me. You must have told everyone to leave me alone."

"We did it on our own!" LJ said.

I turned so slowly that it felt like someone had paused the playground like a movie and then played it at a super, super slow speed.

But it was really that I was so shocked that it took everything in me to turn toward LJ.

"What did you say?" I asked.

"We all came to Nadia on our own. She didn't steal us."

"You can't steal friends," Sammy added.

Everyone nodded their heads.

"Yeah, but you can earn them, and you can lose them," LJ said.

When LJ said that, I felt my whole body get hot. I didn't even know what to say.

"That doesn't make sense," I said. "How could I have lost you?"

LJ shook her head. "For me, it was when Mary Ann came to the group. She was the only person you paid attention to."

"No, she wasn't," I said. "She's part of the group, like everyone."

"Except you didn't pay attention to the basketball game on the court."

"She didn't know how to play, so I was just making sure she had fun."

"And you were too busy focusing on your sharing lunch thing to talk to me."

"That wasn't because of Mary Ann. I just couldn't figure out how to cut my sandwich into fifths."

"No, you were focused on having fun with Mary Ann. Because when I tried to talk to you about Nadia stuff after that, you kept asking Mary Ann's opinion, and you only listened to what she had to say." LJ looked down at the grass. "You made me feel like I didn't matter."

"But...but...I didn't do those things," I said.

"Yes, you did," Mary Ann said. "And you did the same thing to me, too. I didn't realize it until LJ left. But once she did, you were so focused on getting her back, you totally forgot about me. All the stuff you'd been doing to make me feel like part of the group, you completely stopped doing. And if I disagreed with you about Nadia stuff, you didn't want to hear it."

My head wouldn't stop shaking back and forth.

"It's not true!" I said. Then I turned to Sammy, Allana, and

Dale. "So what, you three think I ignored you, too? Because that definitely isn't true!"

Sammy crossed his arms. "I care about my friends. And when you were being mean to LJ, I didn't like it."

Allana and Dale nodded.

You've been so busy
Being mean to Nadia
You didn't realize
You were turning into Nadia

"No offense, Nadia," Allana said. "Just how you used to be. Not how you are now."

Nadia shrugged. "It's okay. I understand."

Sometimes, it's the smallest of things that will make me do something I'm incredibly unproud of. The kind of things I wish I could take back.

Because some of the things I've accidentally done have ended up hurting people, Principal Roberta had me sit with her during recess last week. She taught me how to control my body better.

First, I made sure that nothing was in my hands. I scanned the ground to make sure I wouldn't accidentally bump, stand on, or kick anyone. I wanted to be absolutely 100 percent positive that whatever I did next wasn't going to land somebody in the nurse's office.

Then I said some things that would probably mean I'd be sitting alone at lunch for at least a month.

"WHAT PARALLEL UNIVERSE DID I FALL INTO?" I yelled.

My voice felt scratchy from all the yelling I'd been doing lately. But I still kept yelling.

"You're apologizing to Nadia? You're all trying to tell me I ignored you and I turned mean? You're all just falling right into Nadia's trap! She doesn't like me even an ounce.

And if you all believe her, maybe I don't like any of you an ounce, either!"

I stormed off. I felt like a hot potato that had exploded into a million steaming pieces from being cooked in the microwave for way too long. I couldn't believe what my friends had just said!

Maybe I was better off without any friends.

okay...
Today's officially

THE WORST
DAY
EVER

CHAPTER 12

I stomped my way across the playground. I hoped that by kicking my legs down as I walked, I would let out some of my frustration. It helped a little, but not as much as I'd hoped it would.

When I looked up, I realized

I was at the jungle gym. It looked like a ghost town.

I would have thought that after Nadia (supposedly) stopped charging Bonus Bucks to go down the slide, kids would have been racing to use it. But instead, there wasn't a kid in sight. It's like because it wasn't being taxed, no one even wanted to be on it anymore.

One good thing about that was that it had turned into a really quiet spot where I could be alone.

I climbed up to the top. Then I started running back through everything my friends had just said to me.

First, LJ said that I'd started ignoring her when Mary Ann started hanging out with us. She specifically talked about the basketball game over the weekend.

But LJ was wrong. I hadn't

ignored anybody during that game.

If anything, I'd defended Mary Ann. Everyone else had tried to give her a foul for crashing into LJ, but she didn't know what she was doing. They were the ones being hard on her.

And then LJ and Sammy had gotten their way, because Mary Ann is so nice, and LJ had taken the foul shot and scored on her free throw.

Wait... that wasn't right.

LJ hadn't gotten it in. But that's weird. She always makes her foul shots.

I tried really hard to remember what else happened.

An image popped into my head and my jaw dropped open when I suddenly remembered.

I'm the reason LJ messed up the shot.

And then a lot of other memories from that day came back to me.

Like when Dale tried to pass me the ball, but I was paying attention to Mary Ann.

And when Mary Ann first got there and we immediately did our long handshake and started teaching it to Allana and Dale, interrupting the game.

And the way LJ had looked at me when I left all of them to go hang out with Mary Ann. How I thought it was a weird look but hadn't realized she was feeling hurt because of me.

And then I thought about the

Monday after, and how LJ had tried to talk to me, but I was concentrating so hard on cutting my sandwich for my tradition with Mary Ann that I didn't even look at her.

Okay, LJ *might* have a point about me paying more attention to Mary Ann.

But then LJ wasn't too nice to me after that, either. She had this idea that we should play in Nadia's contest again, and I totally disagreed.

And I had a good reason! Nadia had only ever been absolutely awful to me.

But I started connecting more dots. LJ wasn't *just* mad at me because I had a different idea about the whole Nadia situation. She had already been frustrated with the way I'd been treating her, and this must have added to that. Which must have been why she decided to give up on being friends with me and give Nadia a chance.

It really stunk to think that I was such a bad friend to LJ that she'd rather be friends with Nadia than with me.

And then I realized that *all* of my friends had become friends with Nadia instead of me.

I slouched down on the slide as I thought about Sammy leaving because of how I had treated LJ. But he'd also left because I'd treated him like he was silly for missing her. By the time I wanted to "win" her back, he was already hanging out with her. It could have been easy for me to hear him, to *really* hear him, but I wouldn't listen.

And then there was Mary Ann, who felt just like LJ did. When I was trying to come up with a plan to get LJ back, I was pushing Mary Ann away at the same time.

And then Allana and Dale— why had they left me? They'd been

by my side the whole time.

Oh yeah...right up until I had climbed the very slide I was sitting on and pushed a little kid out of my way. And then yelled about the contest and made it seem like it was all my idea.

Oof. I'd been a real jerk all week.

All this time I'd thought Nadia had become this big friend thief, when it turns out I was just a terrible friend.

Was I as bad as Nadia?

Or, and this was the really confusing question: Was Nadia somehow not that bad? And was I actually worse this week?

I thought back to the very first thing I'd done. I thought about Saturday and the basketball court. There was one thing that could have changed everything, right then and there.

If I'd realized what a jerk I was being, I was pretty sure it would have fixed things every step of the way.

I sat up tall, took a deep breath, and slid down the slide.

It was time for me to take responsibility for this whole situation.

And then the recess bell rang.

I didn't have much time.

CHAPTER 13

"**W**ait!" I yelled.

My old group of friends walked toward the school. None of them turned or stopped.

I'd really, really messed things up with them. That they wouldn't even stop to look at me hurt more than I could have imagined.

I started to tear up. I tried to hold back from crying.

"Please!" I yelled again. "Please, I want to say I'm sorry."

Mary Ann was the first to stop. She looked back at me and I couldn't hold it in any longer. The tears slid down my face.

"Guys, wait," Mary Ann said. "She's serious."

Allana, Dale, Sammy, and LJ turned around. Nadia wasn't with them anymore. They all looked at me with fire in their eyes. It reminded me of last week, when three boys looked at me with the meanest looks I'd ever seen, all because of an accident.

But this was worse. I had accidentally hurt every one of my closest friends.

I cried, heavy. I let the tears stream down my face and fall onto my hoodie.

"I'm so, so sorry," I said. "I realize what a bad friend I was to all of you. I never want to hurt any of you again. I probably will, because I can't seem to stop making mistakes that hurt people. But please know that I never meant to hurt any of you. You're all my best friends."

I took a step forward and turned to each of my friends as I said my apologies.

"Mary Ann, I'm really sorry I stopped paying attention to you. You're my oldest friend, and I don't ever want to lose you again!

"Sammy, I think it was really great that you cared so much about LJ leaving. I wish I'd listened to you.

"Allana, I should have given you credit for the contest. I should have given you credit for the plan to win LJ back. It was your idea, and I should have said that.

"Dale, I'm sorry I dragged you into all of this when you really wanted to stay out of it."

And then I turned toward LJ. I knew I owed her the biggest apology. I wiped my face and tried to take a deep breath before I started.

"LJ, I'm most sorry for the way I treated you. I never meant to push you away. I didn't ever mean for Mary Ann to replace you. I was so excited to have her back as a friend that I let it get in the way of our friendship, and that's just awful. Please, please give me another chance. I won't do it again."

I waited for them to all turn around and walk away. I figured they'd leave me there, crying, because they didn't think I was a very good person anymore and didn't want to be my friends. That they wouldn't accept my apologies.

It started with LJ. She stared at me, and she still looked really mad.

But ... yeah. Thankfully, it didn't stay that way.

Something changed in LJ's eyes, and her face softened. She walked toward me and threw her arms around me, hugging me tight.

Then, all at once, the rest of the group ran at me, and every one of them hugged me, all at once.

Then they all let go of me.

LJ wiped tears off her face. "I'm sorry, too," she said. "Just because I didn't like how you were treating me didn't mean I should have just ignored you. Or been mean back to you."

"Same," Sammy, Allana, Dale, and Mary Ann all said at the same time. Then they all laughed.

"All right, students!" our recess aide, Ms. Harrison, yelled. "Let's get moving to class, please."

There was still one thing that was bugging me, and I knew I had to just be honest with them about it.

"I have one question," I said as we walked back toward the building. "And I'm just telling the truth here, because after last week, I'm just confused. Nadia's like... actually a good person?"

"You know," LJ said, "she's

complicated. She actually told me today that she really did have that fair competition to trick you again. But on Tuesday, after I heard all those rumors, I went over to her and asked her if something was wrong."

I looked at LJ like she'd turned into a bowl of pudding. "You what?"

"I just figured that maybe she didn't really want someone to rule the playground with. Maybe she just wanted a friend."

"A cry for help," Sammy said. "That's what my dad calls it."

LJ laughed. "Anyway, it turns out that wasn't what she started out wanting, but it was also something she was looking for. She's actually pretty funny."

"But what about her tax, and…" I trailed off.

LJ put her hand on my shoulder. She whispered, "Not everybody handles things the right way. I mean, you didn't handle this week all that well, until we told you why we were mad. Nadia stopped taxing after Principal Roberta gave her the in-school suspension. Having nice friends has made a difference, too. She really has changed, Robin."

We walked into the school, and

I saw Nadia up ahead, walking toward Ms. Gaffey's class, too.

And then an absolutely crazy idea popped into my head.

"I'll have to ask my parents when I get home, but is there any way you'd all like to come over to my house tomorrow afternoon?" I took a deep breath. "I'll even invite Nadia."

LJ smiled. Allana and Dale nodded their heads. Sammy looked at LJ smiling, and then he smiled, too.

Mary Ann whispered, "You don't have to invite Nadia, just because she's nicer now. I know you two have a history."

"It's okay," I said. "I'll at least ask her."

It was the right thing to do. I couldn't quite get it straight in my head that Nadia had wanted a friend, but then again, everyone deserves a friend. Even Nadia.

"Hey Nadia!" I said.

I wasn't the least bit surprised that she didn't turn around when I called her name. I ran to catch up to her.

At first it was kind of awkward, and we both just stood there. But then I said, "Do you want to come over to my house tomorrow? Everyone else is coming."

She looked at me like my face was a cookie, and she didn't like cookies any more than she liked me.

"Why are you asking me?" she said. "You don't like me."

It was true, and I couldn't deny it. After everything that had happened between Nadia and me, I couldn't think of her as a friend just like that.

"You're right," I said.

She huffed and began to walk away. I swallowed my pride.

"But maybe that can change," I said.

She stopped and looked back at me. "Really?" she asked. She

smiled this small, tiny, almost-impossible-to-see smile, but I saw it.

"Maybe," I said. "Let's take it one day at a time."

Nadia let the smile grow a tiny bit.

Then it flattened.

"Okay," she said. "But don't think we're going to be best friends. I'm not interested."

I blew out a short breath. "Yeah, me neither," I said.

Jeez, being friends with Nadia was not going to be easy for me.

But I surprised myself when I told her, "But regular friends. That could work."

The small smile creeped onto
her face again.

"Yeah," she said. "Maybe."

I couldn't believe I'd just invited Nadia over to my house. What was I getting myself into?

At least I'd have all of my friends there to help me through it.

And to eat snacks with.

Turns out Nadia hadn't been a friend thief. Now I hoped she wasn't a snack thief. That's a line no one can cross and still be friends with me, that's for sure!

"See you inside," Nadia said, and she ran into Ms. Gaffey's room.

Sammy tapped me on my shoulder.

"Hey, I was thinking about what you said on Saturday," he said.

"Did I say something mean to you?" I asked. "I'm sorry—I don't remember."

"No, nothing like that," he said. "You said we should have a name for our group. I was thinking, what about The Merry Misfits?"

The rest of the group had caught up to us.

"After the week we've had," LJ said, "you really think we're all that merry?"

"Well, we're certainly misfits," Sammy said. "And yeah, I'd say we make each other pretty happy."

"Except when we're hungry," I said. "Then we all need to

stay away from each other until we've eaten."

Everyone laughed as we walked into our classroom.

Merry Misfits. I liked the sound of that.

THE END

CHECK OUT A PREVIEW OF

DIARY OF A 5TH GRADE
OUTLAW
THE BUCKS BANDIT

COMING SOON!

If anyone out there is reading my journal, I bet they think I love Halloween for one reason: Halloween candy.

For the last month, I've

probably written about food at least a hundred times, so I could see why they'd think that.

And sure, candy is great.

But I'm actually not all that into Halloween. My best friend, Mary Ann, and her family usually go on vacation around the end of October, so I don't have anyone to trick-or-treat with. My dad always offers to walk me around, but it feels funny to trick-or-treat without a friend.

Even though I like coming up with scary stories, Halloween scary stories can be really scary. Like, with zombies and vampires being real. That's too much for me.

Plus, I'm not very good at picking out costumes. Kids at my school and in my neighborhood go all out, with fancy face paint and handmade costumes that look like they cost a thousand bucks or something.

And even though my mom and dad are totally nice, we don't have a lot of money for costumes.

But this year, I might change my mind about Halloween.

First of all, Mary Ann's family already went on vacation, so she's around.

Plus, this year, I have a really simple costume that is so cool it's crazy.

A few days ago, Ms. Gaffey, my fifth grade teacher, taught us a really really really old story about this guy named Robin Hood.

As soon as the name came out of my teacher's mouth, a bunch of my friends in the classroom and I all looked at one another.

See, my name is Robin Loxley, but a few weeks ago I earned the nickname Robin Hood. It's mostly because I wear a hoodie like every day to school.

But the similarities don't stop there! Turns out this guy had a bunch of friends he hung out with all the time called the Merry Men.

My friends all call each other the Merry Misfits, because we're a pretty happy group, and we're also a bunch of weirdos, in a good way.

He even used to steal from the rich and give to the poor with his best buddy, Little John! A few weeks ago, my new friend LJ and I basically did the same thing when my former enemy, Nadia, was getting rich by making kids hand over Bonus Bucks—our school's way of rewarding students for doing something good. LJ and I ended up stealing all of the Bonus Bucks from Nadia and returning them to everyone in school.

If Halloween was all about feeling spooky, then the number of ways that Robin Hood and I were the same was extra eerie.

But being Robin Hood also made the perfect costume!

At first, the only part I was worried about was the bow and arrow he used to carry around. I knew Principal Roberta would never let me into the school with something so dangerous.

But I had a perfect fix for that.

Oooh, Dad's calling me for dinner. I'll explain all about it next time I write.

ABOUT THE AUTHOR

Gina Loveless fell in love with kids' books when she was eight and fell back in love with them when she was twenty-eight. She earned her MFA in creative writing from California Institute of the Arts and resides in eastern Pennsylvania.

ABOUT THE ILLUSTRATOR

Andrea Bell is an illustrator and comic artist living in Chicago through the best and worst seasons. She enjoys rock climbing, making playlists, being surrounded by nature, and indulging in video games.